A COLLECTION OF
SHORT STORIES AND POEMS

THROUGH THE VIOLET REDWOODS

XANNA RENAE

First paperback edition October 2021

ISBN 979-8-9850823-0-2 (paperback)
ISBN 979-8-9850823-1-9 (ebook)

NIGHTSHADE
PUBLISHING
Published by Nightshade Publishing
NightshadePublishing.com

THROUGH
THE
VIOLET
REDWOODS

Content Warning

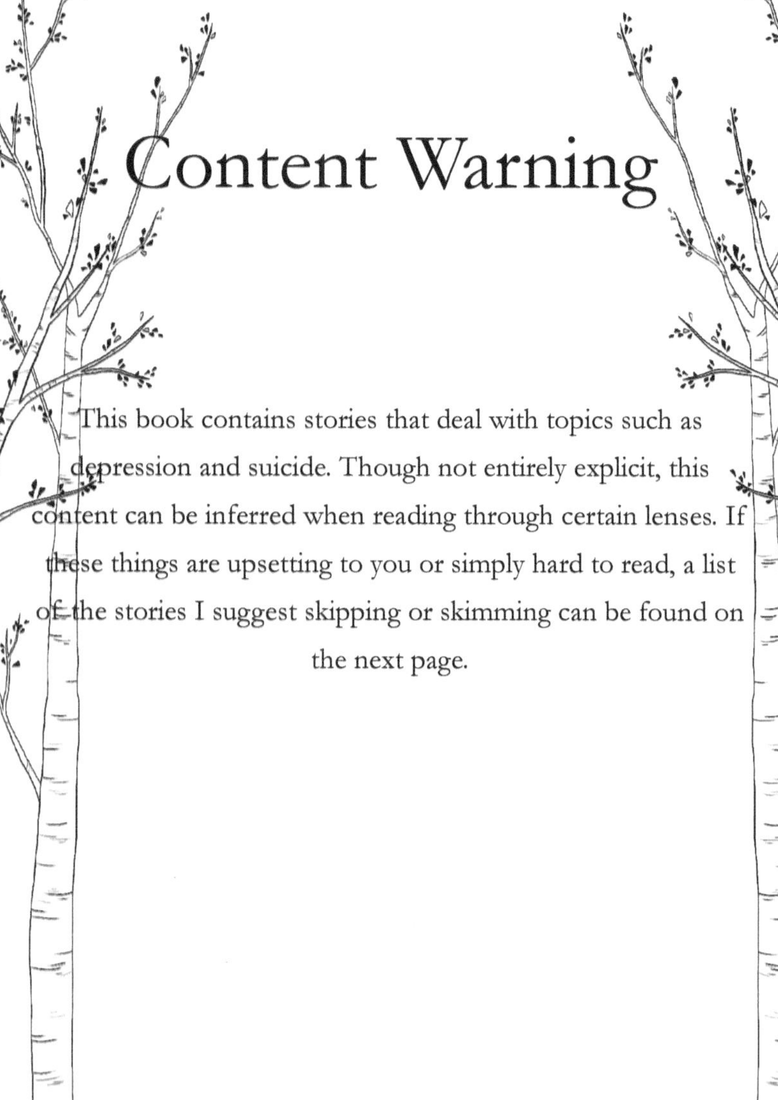

This book contains stories that deal with topics such as depression and suicide. Though not entirely explicit, this content can be inferred when reading through certain lenses. If these things are upsetting to you or simply hard to read, a list of the stories I suggest skipping or skimming can be found on the next page.

Continued Content Warning

The following stories contain content as listed on the previous page. If you wish to remain unaware of the contents of any stories as to keep the element of one's own interpretation, turn the page. Stories are listed below.

Salvation for One

Ground of the Willow Tree

She Ran

Something She Couldn't

Stories

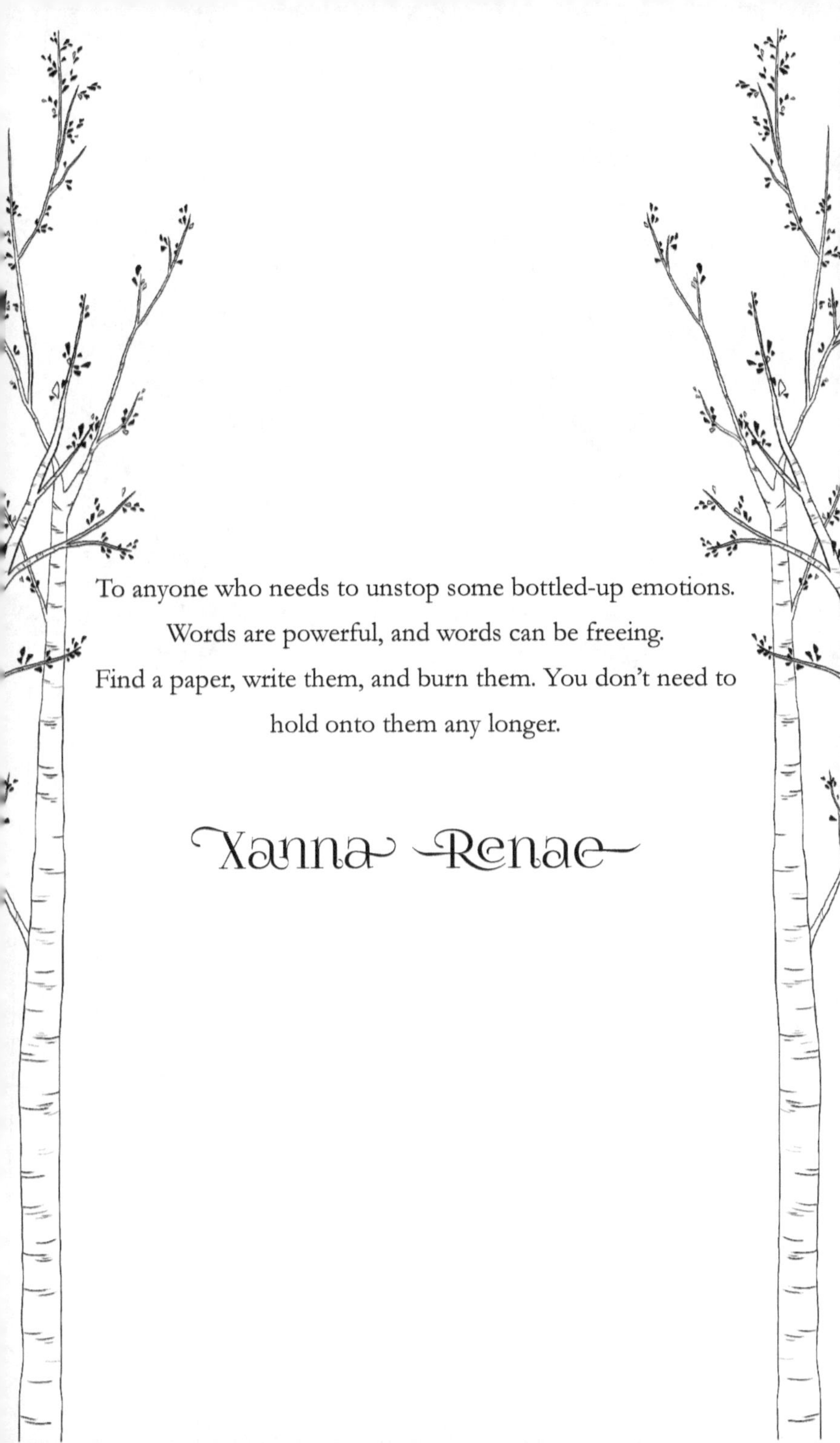

To anyone who needs to unstop some bottled-up emotions.
Words are powerful, and words can be freeing.
Find a paper, write them, and burn them. You don't need to
hold onto them any longer.

Xanna Renae

Pitter Patter

The hall groaned with every step she took away from the door. The chill of the brass knob lingered in one hand as the other hung her purse on the coat rack, which seemingly bent to receive it.

"I'm back." Her voice floated about in the air.

The banister creaked in response, eager for her to set her hand upon it—it would have to wait a while longer. She had business on this floor to attend to first.

The lights burned to life, flickering only half of a half moment. They were eager to please the current Mistress of the home.

The flaking wallpaper curled into a hug on her youthful fingers as she trailed them along the wall. She ducked around a corner, making her way through the archways.

"You're back late." A warm voice curled with the fire in the hearth.

"So sorry, I had a hard time getting away." She shed the

fur coat that swathed her neck and bodice and draped it upon the cabinet to her left. "But I'm here now."

The figure turned around the wings of the velvet chairs, the firelight forming a halo around his face. "My oh my, how horrible." He grinned, his smile stretching over his ivory teeth. His face was the pinnacle of youth and perfection, if one counted imperfections as perfect—which she did. Rolling the stem of a tall glass flute between his long fingers, he took a sip and placed it down on the cocktail table. If the glass was half full, or half empty, she wasn't sure.

"Indeed." She lounged on the tweed chair aside his velvet one. The fire that crackled and popped on just the other side of a mahogany table swathed her. The length of her dress caught up at her knees, a burgundy color. If she thought hard enough she would remember the uneven stitching around the left armhole. But there was grace in remembering that she was still yet learning the craft. She had many years to master the art of sewing.

The man's eyes followed her down as she sat, the smile never letting from his face. He never was able to keep the emotions of happiness at bay within his skin. "What news of town do you bring on your lips? Gossip never quite reaches my ears when I linger in the streets, but it seems to find you in every corner. I'm *almost* jealous."

"Almost? And why is that, my dear?" She gave a smile of her own, resting her elbow on the arm of the chair, and her chin on her palm. Tapping her fingers on her cheek in a lazy manner.

"Because it would rob me of hearing it from you, and that's all the more exciting." He cooed, leaning back to rest in his chair now that she had finished perching herself and intended to stay a while.

"Perhaps with a cup of something to drink I would let loose my lips, but for now they are oh so dry and cannot afford to move." She looked to the wooden archway that led to the rest of the house, it was hand carved around the edges with both purposeful and accidental marks. Each brought its own charm.

The small dent from the heels she wore on her wedding stood proud against the left side, the kisses shared upon it imprinted only in her mind.

Looking back, the cocktail table now held two glasses, one half full or half empty, and one completely full with bubbles and laughter. The stem of the glass was cool in her fingers as she plucked it.

She leaned over and poured a drop or three into the fire, offering her thanks to those that serve.

"Well. . .Mrs. Var had her baby. A girl. Nearly a full head of blonde hair from what I've heard. She is already a beauty."

"All children are in your sight."

"Yes, well, children are blank. They are completely themselves, yet to have taken on any parts of anyone else. Or to have given up parts. They are perfect. And cute—we mustn't forget the fact that children are cute, my love."

He picked up his glass and tilted it towards her. "To the new child. May she stay as whole as she can be, and only take

on the best of others."

She smiled and drank. "You always have the best toasts."

He chuckled.

The woman curled both hands around the stem of the glass and took a look about the room. The corners of the small sitting room would need dusting soon. Its eight-legged occupants would first need taken to the garden. Hopefully they would make a home out there instead of venturing back inside.

She slipped out of her heels and rested her ankles, crossed, upon the small table. The man let out a low hum at the action but made no move to stop her.

"And what shall we do?" She asked, taking another sip.

"What is it that needs to be done, my dear?" He looked at her, brows furrowing.

She tapped her nails against the glass. "The empty room upstairs, the cream one. It houses nothing of importance. But the room begs to hold something of great value." She met his gaze and smiled.

He smirked and raised an arm behind his head as a rest. "Great importance? I'll have to think. We could move the bookshelf? Books are quite important."

He laughed as she stood from her seat and quickly crossed over to join him in the velvet chair. "Not important enough for what I'm thinking. Something less filled to completion. Something that would need to grow. That sounds right to me." She tapped at his nose.

He sat up, brushing his nose against hers. "I feel as though

you already have an answer, to which I am eager to listen." The house creaked in agreement. A small draft running down the stairs, a set of clacking on the marble floor in the kitchen, and a few scrapes against the grand windows.

She hoped the sounds of little pittering and pattering would soon come with coos and laughs.

"How eager are you to listen, my love?"

Pretend

Every night I'd pass by, convinced that they were there. The little creaks and small puffs against my heels from things ever hidden. Stares branded into my skin. There was no getting away from the things I had no idea of. I'd look and I'd scour. Searching for any trace of their existence. Any shred of evidence left behind by the monsters that poked at the back of my mind. But nothing showed itself. And now that I'm older and I know they are there. . . I simply convince myself that they are not.

A Letter to my Lost

She ran her fingertips over the paper, yellow along the edges and scratched on the face from dragging the nib of her dry pen over it. Tracing her would be sentences before setting them in ink.

They evaded her. Leaving her wondering how to start the words that longed to burst from her chest like a dove in a cage.

A few pairs of footsteps circled and echoed about her in the old library. Dust covered most of the aged books that lined the shelves, and the rest of them were filled with modern tellings of stories whose origins were long forgotten. All of these words were able to be written, but the ones within her refused to let her alone and be freed.

There were a million different ways that one could start a letter.

But she couldn't find any of them as she footslogged through her head.

So she stood and started over to the grand shelves to her left.

Pen still poised in her hand, she started twirling it about. A nifty, albeit useless, trick she picked up.

Her legs enjoyed the last bits of light that the grand windows let in. The skirt she wore hit just at her knees, a scandalous bit of fashion that was making its way into the world.

The worn leather spines were refreshing on her fingertips. She plucked a book free, skimming the words over the course of a few pages. Hoping she'd find her own words there. She found only the words of others, which was to be expected.

Perhaps the words escaped her because writing a letter to someone who was lost was pointless? Her mind could not conjure the words to fit her feelings in the end, there was no point. The recipient was gone.

She wandered from classic literature to poems, and still found nothing. Artbooks held no answers, nor the atlases— aside from giving her more places she could run away and hide in. The coasts looked promising.

They had spoken about going there once. Buying a house painted a deep green with pine along the edges. A small kitchen and space for a family to grow. Whispered promises of dancing with the waves that crashed against the cliffs on breaths that the wind had stolen from her.

The thought stopped her from making the next stride.

Maybe—just maybe the breath in their lungs had made it to all the places they had planned to see?

That was a comforting thought.

They had made it.

The pen almost fell from her hands. She needed to tell him that.

Her skirt fluttered and flapped behind her as the shoes she wore clacked upon the marble floors like horses in a race.

She dipped her pen into the little well of ink she had picked off of the librarian's desk and scrawled the date in the upper corner.

Now there was nothing left to do but bleed.

Time of Saturn

It is said time heals all wounds.

Spoken as if Saturn himself would come down bearing tools in a belt of rings and stitch me back together. Time should heal me.

Time aged me.

The aches burrowed deeper as each moment passed. My body was stiff with an age my years did not reflect.

Time cares not for how I feel, he pushes me further into pain and longing. My wounds would not heal.

Time has forsaken me.

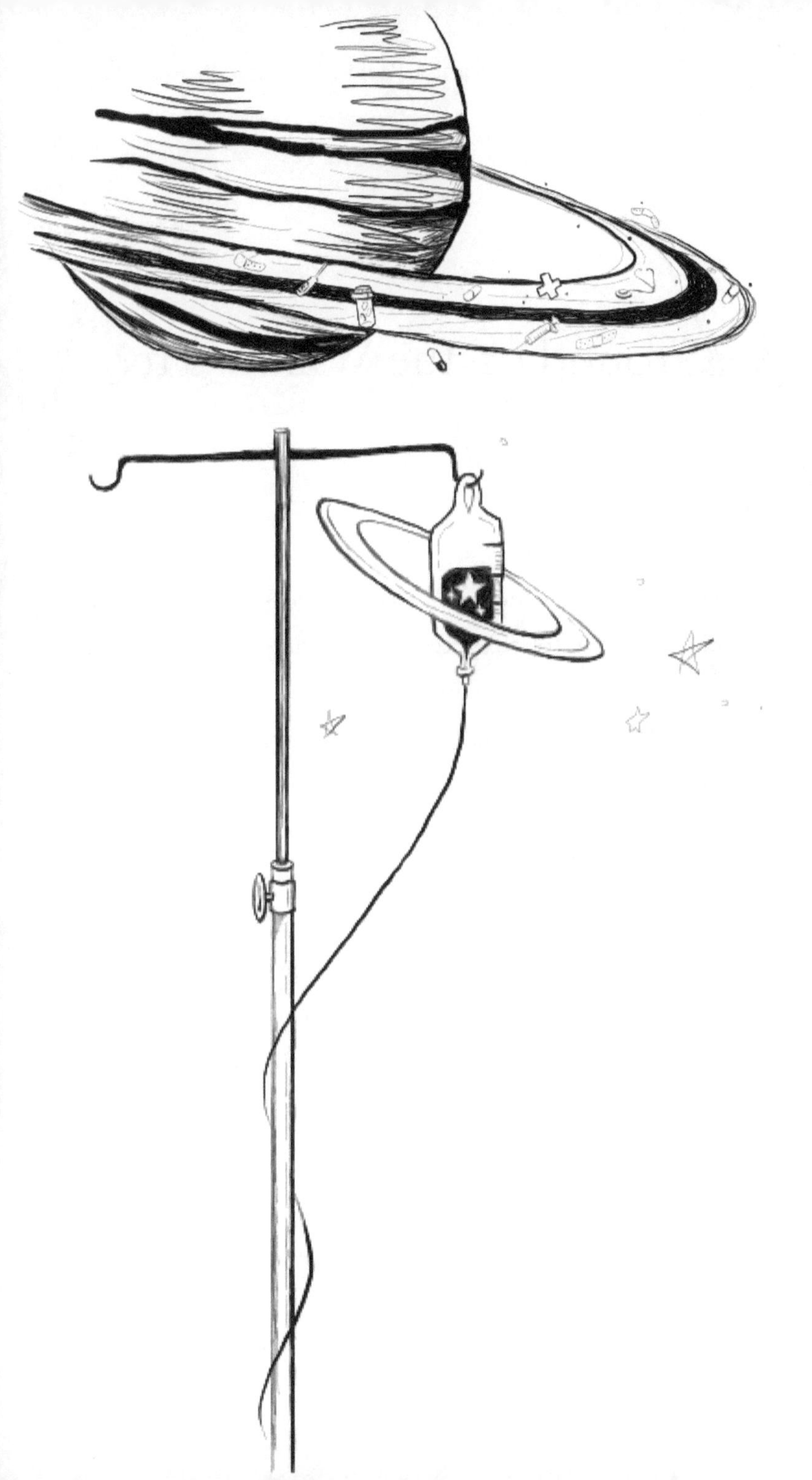

Ground of the Willow Tree

The bark of the willow tree was rough under her fingers as she found purchase. Hoisting herself into the branches wasn't an easy task, but it was done all the same. With huffing and puffing, she climbed and climbed as the leaves sunk down all about her.

For a tree with such a sad name, it brought her great joy. How the little bees would fly about in the early spring, the boughs dancing with a rare summer breeze. She supposed she felt a lingering sadness when fall came and stole all the leaves away, leaving the tree naked and cold, lying upon the earth. But winter came quickly with sicknesses and a blanket to cover the tree from her eyes.

The tree was her constant companion, one she couldn't find fault in, though she was unsure if the tree could speak the same. Unspeakable things were whispered to the sticks and unfathomable deeds plotted with the gnarled knolls upon the trunk. Words better left unspoken weighed on the

branches. Pulling tears from the leaves.

The tree was a keeper of many a thing. Locks of doll hair that were plucked and kept by the willow from summers long ago, and stolen kisses peppered when the canopy was thick with shade. Her life was tied to the tree, the thought of her very being was conceived in the shade. It made sense then, for her to leave from the shade.

The ground was far less forgiving than the tree had been.

13

War Painter

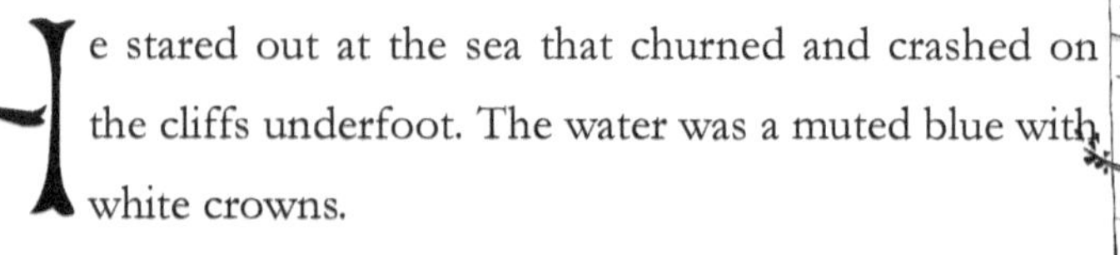

He stared out at the sea that churned and crashed on the cliffs underfoot. The water was a muted blue with white crowns.

The ocean reigned supreme here—all and one must bow to the waves.

A cry sounded from the sky as the tempest rolled in and demanded to be acknowledged. This war came often in this season. The two fought, unable to see how perfectly they blended together.

So he did his best to capture it.

Sat upon his chair, a tarp above his head and a brush in hand, he swept the waves into the heavens with azurite. Lightning created a web of lights upon the face of the waters that were gone before he could trace it. Its imprint lasted when he closed his eyes, that would do well enough.

He squinted, his eyes darting between the painting and life. More green paint would be needed to match the waters.

It was going well thus far. Maybe a truce could finally be found in the combined beauty of disaster?

A ship made its way into the scene and the man wondered if he should allow it to root itself in with ocher. He hoped it wouldn't become a victim in this battle of dominance.

The waves changed their pattern. He took to stippling in the clouds—they didn't seem to have any plans on leaving. Dabs of cadmium upon splotches of white.

Lightning struck closer upon the water, climbing up the cliffs. His nerves were alit—but he couldn't stop.

The battle had only just begun.

Behind Glass

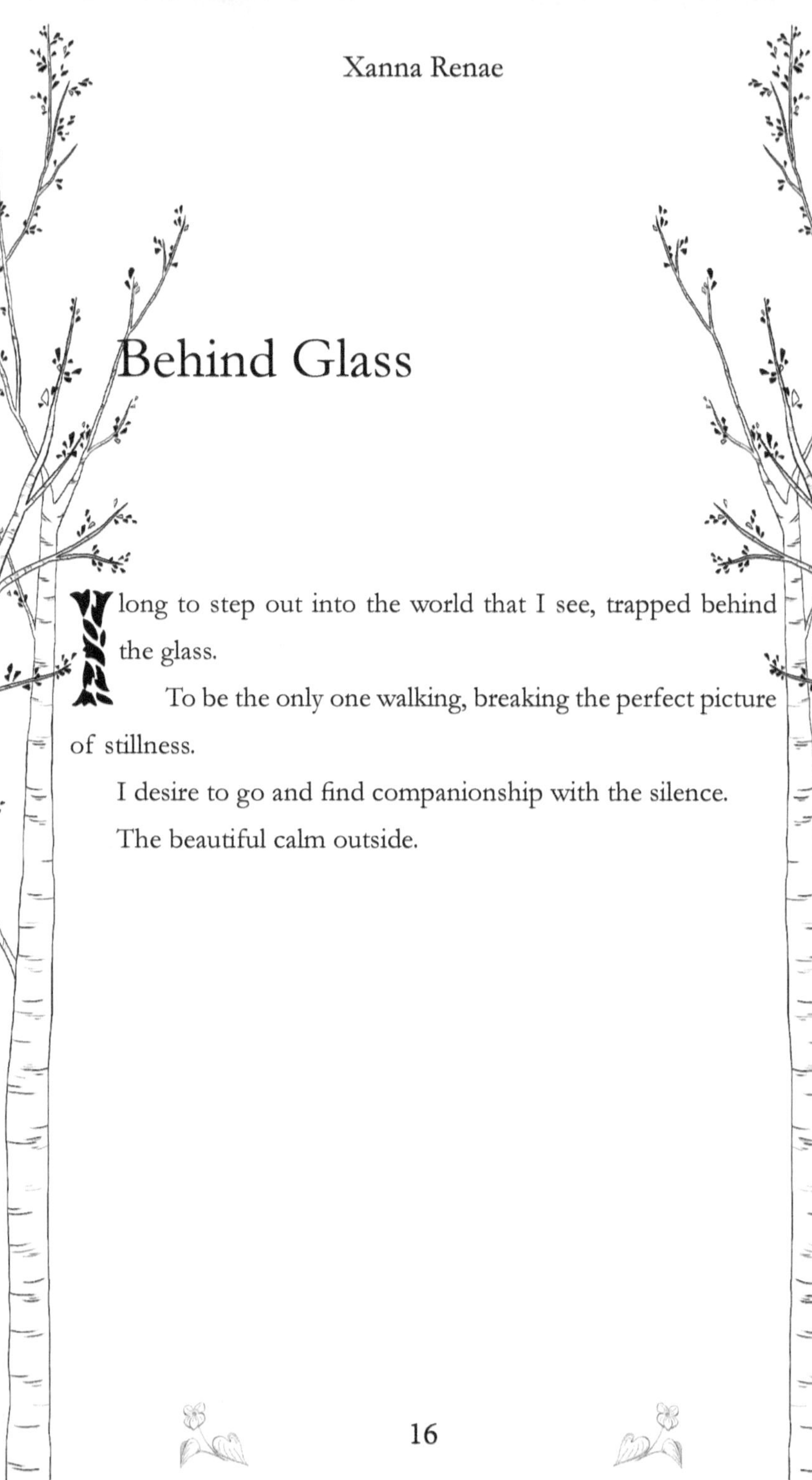

I long to step out into the world that I see, trapped behind the glass.

To be the only one walking, breaking the perfect picture of stillness.

I desire to go and find companionship with the silence.

The beautiful calm outside.

Join Thee

Were it not so bitter cold I'd join thee in this night.

But longingly I'll watch you here until the morning light.

Monster in my Closet

It grew until it burst through hinges,
biting a path through flesh into open air.
It frightened everyone who encountered it,
unrecognizable as it consumed my being.
I begged and pleaded for it to listen;
compliance was not its mission.
Its course was laid in fire and brimstone,
raging until everything was devoured.
And only once the beast was sated,
Could it be dragged back inside.
I checked the locks, reframed the door,
unwilling to suffer anymore.
I pressed it away, deep, deep down,
willing to forget it there.
A monster lives inside of me;
I check it oft' to watch it lie.
Yet, sometimes I cannot tell

when it is there

and I am here.

Death of Light

I write for my fairy lights, wrapped in ivy. Watching them shine is all I desire.

Their glow enchants me, and the wires on which they burn wrap around my heart, binding me to their beauty. I could never let go of the strands which fuel me.

I write for their enjoyment of life. For if words do not come, then power they cannot receive.

Clotted Feelings

er fingers moved across her laptop's keyboard in an untraceable rhythm as her thoughts waxed and waned. Several emotions swirled to life within her. Anger blinded her with the brightness of her screen, sorrow slowed her fingers, anxiety had her peering out the window to make sure that no prying eyes could follow her movements as she bled her thoughts.

Betrayal demanded she act. Grace stilled her.

She bit her lip, ripping off another flake of dried skin, wincing slightly as it pulled at live flesh.

She hated her kindness. It was oft a tool that was wielded against her by her own hand at the will of others. She ripped out her heart at the thought of causing another pain. Killing herself in the process of keeping someone else's peace.

Was it right?

Was it wrong?

Her mind was split on the matter.

The waters outside the window churned with the passing storm, she wished it had stayed. The thunder could take away her rage and the lightning could have given her a flash of hope. Nature stood against her as well.

She looked about the room. She couldn't see anything with the lights off, aside from the screen with black words she didn't even want to be writing. She wanted to be sleeping, peacefully lulled by the soft sound of breathing and the snuggles of a cat. But in this instance, they were gone.

She felt foolish. She knew they would return, but a part of her whispered that they were gone forever. And she couldn't sleep with the thought of reality and normality having changed. She needed patterns. She needed assurance.

Today, she received only a cold back from a warm heart. It was an apathy she wasn't prepared for.

She had crawled her way to safety only to be spat upon and cast aside by the bringers of it.

It hurt. It was painful.

Logic said she should harden herself with it. Don it as a set of blackened armor that would keep her from harm.

Her own nature said to bear it and try once more.

Again, everything seemed split. And she was caught between two sides of a tug of war that could only end in ripping her in half.

She didn't fancy that idea.

What alternative did she have? She either buried it or bore it upon her chest as a shield.

22

The moon sat behind the clouds. No answers would come from the bringer of sleep, for it too had forsaken her. She had forgotten that.

She would remember it this time.

She should have slept hours ago, before it all happened. It wouldn't have had the chance to root so deep within her, a weed that took air from her lungs and stole the light from her heart.

She should sleep.

She had medicine that could force it upon her, but the thought of one more thing being out of her control was terrifying and she couldn't face that. She didn't want to face anything.

Where had it come from?

It came from nowhere, and everywhere. It was sudden, she hadn't the time to prepare.

But now, in the dead of night, she did. She would stay awake until morning came with an apology upon the lips of pain, and she would accept it for love and the inability to cause trouble. She didn't like trouble.

She didn't like these feelings either.

Another split. She should roll a die—two, just to be fitting to the feelings she had. Two dice and the rolls would be her fate. . . if she believed in things like that.

She didn't have dice anyways.

Street lamps cast an orange hue in a straight line towards her on the lake. It was silly, but in a way, it scared her, and also brought out the feeling of humor. Either way, again with the splits, she would dismiss it with the oncoming wave of

nothingness in her spirit.

What should she feel next? What should she try and process?

Anger wanted to arise again, and hopefully come out victorious this time. It wouldn't. She refused to give in to anger. The messages she deleted as she typed them were proof of that concept.

But now she had to pick something else to occupy her mind, lest it wander too far into the intrusive darkness that sat at the edges of her vision, beckoning her come.

She wouldn't listen.

She turned her music up louder. That would do.

But now she'd been sat for far too long and she couldn't think of another thing to type. The feelings had been bled, at least for a little while. Perhaps sleep was willing to accept her now that she had cried again?

She was afraid of going back to her bed to try. It was too hot in there anyways, and far too alone.

She liked being alone, but it was also the thing she hated the most. She wanted to pick when to be alone. Now was a time she hadn't picked.

Opposites, contrast, all the things once more. How many parallels can one feel in the span of an hour before they burst? Was she willing to try and figure it out? Or would it lead to her pressing send like she almost had so many times?

She didn't want to think about pressing send on the messages where she poured out her raw feelings. It wouldn't be fair to anyone but her, and that wasn't fair. She had to consider

everyone else before herself and she was going to explode.

She turned her music up more.

She wondered if the feelings were done yet. If they had lifted the claws they sunk into her flesh. It was a rotten feeling. A sickening sweet smile followed with being left behind.

It was foolish.

She would feel foolish come morning.

But it was still night, solate into the night that it was almost morning. The feelings had merged already. Interesting.

She looked at the orange line again, the street light that cast it. The windowpanes on the balcony doors perfectly highlighted the light. Perfect lines.

She liked perfect things. They were easy to look at and brought a sense of peace. There was peace in chaos as well.

Again with the opposites.

She turned up her music.

It wouldn't go any louder this time.

A seductive melody played in her ears, tempting her to do what her heart desired. She didn't know what her heart wanted.

Earlier it had wanted a cookie.

She wasn't given the chance to buy a cookie. That hurt.

Then her body fell apart and she sobbed alone.

And now the sadness was back, it hadn't been properly dealt with before.

Maybe none of this would have happened if she had gotten a cookie, or if she hadn't been hushed, or if people spoke feelings instead of nothingness that confused her and

left her alone in the middle of the night typing on her laptop.

She had a lot of feelings that she was sure would have been solved with a cookie.

It was a good cookie too, not something she could get when the sun rose. It would be a Sunday, and the shop would be closed. She knew she wasn't getting a cookie on Monday either, or Tuesday, or any other day of the week for weeks. It was a simple request too.

All the things she felt today could have been solved, for they were all simple requests.

Listen to me when I speak, I have the answer.

Talk to me please, I need my best friend.

I would really like a cookie right now.

No, no, no.

Maybe she was being pathetic?

What stage of grief was she in now? Could she even remember them all? Let's see.

Disbelief, denial—were those the same? Anger, bargaining, acceptance. Mourning was in there somewhere. She had slipped back into it, so she knew for a fact that it belonged in the group. That's six, were there seven? Or only five? When would she move into acceptance?

It sounded scary, she didn't want to accept what had happened. She had been wronged in so many ways by people and her own body.

She was so tired. She wanted to give up.

Was that acceptance?

Just wanting it all to end? It didn't seem like an uplifting place to end. Accepting things like this seemed dangerous, like she would continue to let people step all over her. She had grown so used to just letting it happen.

A notification popped up, she hoped it was a message filled with apologies.

Someone, an acquaintance, shared a photo.

She looked back to the orange glow. Maybe it held some kind of answer that she was seeking?

That was a stupid thought.

It was a light that shone for everyone the moment it was placed in the ground. It wasn't a beacon of hope for her, not a lighthouse for her in the misty sea of her emotions. Stupid thought.

What stage of grief were those lines? She was getting angry at herself for feeling hopeful—she had said it: anger. Easy answer. If only others could have given her those sorts of answers too. That was anger as well.

She wished she could do today over. She would change so many things. This outcome wasn't worth it, and she wasn't far enough into the future to understand how this night would shape her. It didn't matter at this point. She would sleep and wake up and it would be the day over again!

She would give a few pep talks, smile a bit more perhaps? She wouldn't eat the same thing for lunch, that's when she'd started feeling unwell. Or was it before lunch? She was always sick so she was never sure what caused what and when something did or didn't react this time.

React reminds her of how babies react to things, which brings her back to how she hates being babied. She knows what she can and can't do, no one else seems to understand that.

An ad interrupted her music. She didn't go to skip the ad, she didn't care enough.

The feelings were raw, and she needed to use the bathroom. But the bathroom was in the direction of the bed, and she would feel inclined to sleep if she went that way, and she still hadn't sorted her feelings, so many pages, so little sorting.

She was less angry, she knew that. But only slightly less angry. She debated not speaking tomorrow in the fear that the anger would pour over again and she would bite someone's head off, which seemed appealing at the moment. So that meant it was a very bad idea. She wouldn't do that no matter how badly she wanted to.

Maybe she still would. Living with anger isn't good, but taking anger out on others, no matter how deserved she thought it was, wasn't something she wanted to do. Her feelings were lesser than those of others. She didn't have the right to want to express things when they didn't care and she knew it.

She thought they cared, but then the line came.

I don't care.

It hurt. It hadn't been phrased in such a direct way as that, but it was at the same time.

She had poured out her hurt and pain and was told by her comforter that it didn't matter.

Anger and sadness were fighting for custody of her soul.

And she needed to use the bathroom.

She stopped caring.

She was done. This was pointless to a degree, like a dull pencil. It was useful in some way, but wasn't as nice as a mechanical one.

She needed to pee.

She would stop bleeding into her keys.

Until she started up again. But for now, she decided she would stop emoting.

Her feelings had clotted.

Ostrich Thinking

Breath bled out of my lungs as the last waves of shock ran out through my toes.

I was wrong. Foolish—thinking too lightheartedly. Perhaps if I were not a woman I would be seen as smart? But, because I am delicate as a flower, I need to study more.

I needed to get my head out of the clouds and hide it in the dirt.

Midwest Moon

lice huffed as she bent and rested her elbows on her knees. "If you don't stop moving so fast, my legs are going to fall off. And I doubt that I'll grow a new body, no matter how magical you say these woods are." Her flashlight cut through the bushes, scanning the trees and plants.

A squirrel ran up a trunk and jumped through the leaves.

She wiped her brow and straightened, fixing her flashlight on the areas she actually wanted to be looking. Like the path Will was trotting away on.

You punk.

Will's stance grew shorter as he continued on without her. Alice glared at him; she hoped he could feel the murderous intent of it.

The large pack on his back bounced around like a toddler. "We're going to miss it if you keep stopping us, Al!" He called back. Not at all minding what a disrupting presence he was to the forest around him. The creatures that lurked didn't take well to their sleep being stolen from them—they were quick to rip it back.

Alice grumbled under her breath, unwilling to make the same arguments over and over. The meteors would still be there when they reached the top. Nothing would change that fact.

Daring a look up she started walking again, noting how thick the canopy seemed. Leaves overlapped branches that seemed as thick as her neck. Alice wasn't sure that the sky would ever break through again to pull her out of the darkness.

"I'm coming, I'm coming." Alice called back—softer than he had. She wasn't sure what could be listening.

She kept marching, shaking off the slime that trickled down her spine.

"I can't believe that the weather worked out so well." Will bounced with each step. The four cups of coffee, grape-flavored energy drink, and sacrifice to the gods had wired him for the long night to come.

"You did remember to pack the tent away in all of that, right?" Alice stared at his back, doing her best not to look past it.

It was hard to believe all they would need for a night was packed away in there. A tent, pillows, water, food, instant noodles—too processed to be considered food, but too important to leave out according to their stomachs. The sleeping bags were rolled up and resting on her back along with a few extra pillows.

She felt like a little turtle. Maybe she would be considered a painted one with her pastel hair? A bird cawed and suddenly

she remembered that birds ate turtles. "I'm not a turtle." She whispered as she drew her shoulders up to her chin.

"What? I thought we were gonna sleep with the sky as our tent. . . no worries, I'm joking." Will held his hands up, almost shielding his face from her as if she would slap him. She had half a mind to.

"Good. If you hadn't, I'd march right back down this stupid mountain."

Will shot a little knowing, smug, grin at her. "No you wouldn't."

"I wouldn't risk being taken by some monster to see a few pretty stars." She shot back.

Though her words were said in jest, she feared what repercussions would come from speaking them to the wind. Perhaps a faraway monster would be swept up in a gale and brought here just because she said something.

Alice cursed internally.

Something grabbed her foot, gravity forsook her as the creature took hold. The wind cut against her face and her knees stung as the packed dirt and loose stones scraped against her knees and shin. The air in her lungs burned with a scream that was ready to belt into the air. The monster turned her ankle, a popping sound accompanying it.

"Woah! Girl you've gotta be careful. These tree roots are pretty gnarly." Will's hand reached down towards her, blurred in her vision by tears that welled up.

She looked down and, true to his word, a twisted root

protruded from the ground. "Right. Tree root." The words came out pitched in a laugh.

"Don't tell me you thought it was a—"

Alice glared at him, pointing her flashlight up at her face. "Finish those words and they'll be your last." She rubbed her ankle. It had popped, but no damage was done.

Will simply laughed and finished pulling her to her feet. His hands were warm, slightly rough from the time he spent buffing and repairing old arcade machines. The old parts had a way of snagging him as if they didn't want to be closed back up in their case.

Perhaps she was being a bit dramatic.

Alice let out another laugh as she bent down and patted off her knees. Thankfully nothing came back on her fingers. She would still disinfect them when they set up camp, but the forest hadn't drawn first blood.

"Here, why don't we walk arm in arm?" He looped his arm through hers, allowing her a moment to switch the flashlight to her other hand before they started off. "This way if any scary tree roots try snatching you up again I can fight them off for ya." His smile was soft, the indent of a dimple started to form on his left cheek.

"Smooth talker." She mumbled as she nestled further into his side. "How far have we hiked?"

When they'd picked out the spot to camp a few weeks ago it was in the agreement that the destination be no further than four miles away from their car, a nifty hybrid that saved bank on

gas. Which made it a blessing for Will to drive through half the state for repair jobs.

"Well," he coughed and scratched the back of his head. Alice wondered if he knew that was his tell for bad news. If anything, it always gave her time to brace herself for whatever was coming. "We've been climbing at a steady pace, I'd say we've only got a little while longer to go." Will looked down at his watch. He nodded but said nothing else.

She smiled up at him. "I guess that just gives us more time to talk and walk."

And talk they did. Conversation smothered her frazzled nerves with every step they took. Alice didn't even mind when Will jostled her a bit and pretended as though a beast had snatched him up from behind. She did slug his shoulder for good measure.

The leaves rustled in the distance, Alice hoped it was just a deer. Running season was fast approaching.

She looked through the leaves, trying to see a glimpse of something nice with her light. But the ways the branches twisted were frightening. Faces grew in the trunks of the trees and a peal of sinister laughter twisted her stomach as it rode on the wind.

She couldn't do this. They had to go back. They had to—

"We've arrived!"

She lifted her head and gasped. The trees parted like pages in a book and opened up to the vastness of space.

The sky was a deep navy bleeding to black. Stars were littered about and in the middle of it all was the moon.

It rose full and bright into the stars. The light of it pushed the shadows of the woods behind her.

Her shoulders and hands relaxed, she hadn't even noticed the tension building in them. Alice ran past Will into the clearing, basking in the glow.

Wildflowers grew around the edges of the campsite, black-eyed Susans, honeycombs, delphinium, and several other bushes with little white specks.

"It's beautiful." She turned and looked at him, her nose brushing the side of his.

He grinned, the skin around his eyes wrinkling, then he wrapped her in a hug. As best as one could hug in all the gear they wore. His voice was warm against her neck. "I told you so."

She pulled back to glare at him.

"I'm starving." He groaned and patted her shoulder before jogging into the clearing and throwing his pack to the ground.

"Careful, don't break the Switch!" Alice ran forward to check on the console. Another necessity she decided on bringing. She sat and started digging through the pack to find it.

Will plopped down beside her and started organizing everything. "Relax, it's in a case. So, I was thinking ramen for dinner?" Will shook the two red packages about with an unnecessary intensity, a wild look on his face

"You know what? I'm fine with that" Alice laughed, leaning back on her hands to better bask in the comforting light of the moon.

Moonlit Play

The trees swayed with the song in the wind. The setting sun was chased by the cool of night. Purples and pinks joined blue in a dance in the sky. And the moon rose steadily over the horizon to glimpse the last breath of its companion.

Frogs and crickets struck up a new tune, accompanying the wind. The fireflies lit the scene. And if one looked carefully, a fairy or two could be spotted playing near tables of mushrooms and rings of rocks.

The potted flowers shed golden dust as accessories for all who wandered near. And the fox lay still and silent for anyone who wandered far. The moon watched over all, keeping a tally of nature's play.

And when the moon grew tired, and the musicians lost their beat, everyone would lay down a while as the moon sunk low. Waiting for the warmth of the sun to bring a new game to play. And the cycle would repeat and repeat and repeat.

She Ran

She ran as fast as she could, but life always had a way of catching up with her. Smacking her into the dirt.

Being surrounded by others was horrible, so she distanced. Hoping, praying that it would somehow make things less painful, more bearable. But it was just the same.

Because others were not the problem, she was. She couldn't outrun herself, but oh how she had tried.

She tried everything that existed under the sun. Swimming, biking, knitting, drinking. She tried tattoos and prayer, drugs and gardening.

But nothing erased the fact that she was still herself. That life was still happening though she tried to drown it out.

She threw herself into school and earned victory. She let herself stop caring and wallowed in loss.

But still, she was herself.

She had tried everything.

Now she found herself at the end of a rope.

My Dearest

The temple organ had been singing a beautiful dark tune for days on end, and no one could find a rhyme or reason for it. Priests had tried incense and chants, herbs and animal blood. Things like that would work on a small spirit, maybe even a ghost of moderate standing. Nothing made the playing stop. And then more things started going wrong.

This was a bit bigger than that. She wasn't sure what it was—*yet*. But Lysa would find out soon enough, she was sure.

"I know that you're here, why don't you come out and play?" Lysa's hand curled about the wooden pike nestled in her leather satchel. It was an excellently crafted bag, always nice and cool to the touch in the hot months, and warm in the cold months. An enchanted gift from a merchant she saved from a cursed lamp.

She *also* got the lamp.

The temple was cold—an unnatural cold. A good sign that this wouldn't end up a prank by some mischievous kids. She would be receiving payment. Her stomach growled in

agreement with the thought.

The splinters of the pike threatened to pierce through her leather gloves. She needed to be careful.

The minor chords switched to major as the piece ended. *Picardy third.* Always unsettling, but always so satisfying.

The lungs of the organ hummed, no keys or peddles colliding with the ground this time. A cool wind burst from the pipes. She staggered on her feet.

"That's not a nice way to play." Lysa let her eyes trail about the room.

From where she stood, bathed in the moonlight let in from the colored windows of the saints and the glow of at least two hundred candles, she could see almost everything.

It was the perfect spot for a pulpit, really. A priest could make out anything and everything that happened in the sanctuary from the spot. She was thankful she asked the pulpit be moved for the night. It wasn't something she needed in her way, as with the priests that requested to be present during her time here. The collateral damage that could happen with someone else being present was far too high.

She would have asked the same of the altar if she didn't think the priests would die of shock by the request.

Laughter rang through the room, close to that of a child's tune. She narrowed her eyes, it had fled behind her, closer to the altar than she already was. A dangerous place for a crpy to reside. The wooden pike was useless—for now. Unexpected visitors were always making themselves known to her during times like this.

But now she knew what she was up against. The clues fit.

The haunting had started off simple, she was told. Things that were hard to notice at first. Candles burning far too quickly and far too dim. Wrinkles in the carpets that moved like snakes. The toilets had run dry, and there was a crack in every mirror that entered the building. A crpy made sense now that she thought about it, but the possibility of a wift was still too great in her mind. Crpy's were mischievous little creatures, the souls of fae who were killed somehow. Their spirits remained in the living realms. They loved to cause problems.

Lysa pulled out the ornate compact from her bag, a useful item when going up against a gorgon. It cracked along the bottom right, branching out like a sapling in the spring.

She nodded to herself. A crpy indeed. What bad luck for her, she liked this mirror.

Purple shot out behind her. She dropped the compact, not minding how it shattered on the ground and crunched under her feet. Hands now free, she dug into her bag fast as she could, feeling for the small, cool, pearl stopper, *where was the pearl stopper?*

Mother of pearl was the only substance that didn't corrode when it came into contact with the flurn powder. And she couldn't find it.

"Blast it!" She tossed her bag off and made for the altar herself. "You're not the victor here, buddy." She jumped atop the table, not minding the golden goblets and books that were stacked upon it, nor the candles that burned upon the carpet now. That damage could be remedied with no effort.

Crpy's were susceptible to two things in this realm: flurn powder, made from pure silver mixed rose petals, and a mixture so dark she would never reveal its contents to anyone; and crosses, just like the one perched atop the Saints Scepter.

"Milady, you mustn't! It cannot be touched by mortal hands!" A priest's voice called from the doors of the sanctuary she was sure she had locked.

She dared a look back as a shot of purple flew straight for the old man. Once possessed, the only option for ridding the host of the creature was sending the soul to the holy realm. She didn't fancy murdering an old man. Her lungs were ready to heave a cry, arm raised in an attempt to tell the man to flee.

"Indeed, darling. It wouldn't be becoming of you to do such a thing." Velvet draped over her skin as words flooded her ears. Her neck crunched as it curled in upon itself, trying to force the voice out.

"By the heavens, what is that?" The old man shook as a leaf in a tempest, the purple mist froze.

A shadow cast down from the pipe organ. Perched upon the top, tapping the pipes with long fingers was a creature far fouler—and far more powerful than the crpy.

"Well done. You have served your purpose." The purple mist was gone with the throw of his arm.

"Priest, I advise you, return to your quarters. This is a dangerous creature—"

"How rude of you Lysara, I haven't even the chance to say hello." He grinned at her and taking hold of one of the golden

pipes, slid down to the ground. His black leather shoes crunched on the red velvet carpet. The room fell several degrees as he strode closer, and her blood began to boil.

"Leave." She commanded. The old man ran, not before sealing the sanctuary doors and casting a blessing upon them. She felt the wave of purity rush past her. She wouldn't be able to open the door without a large amount of concentration and luck.

How kind of him.

"I take it the crpy was your doing?" She glared as he approached.

His hair ran like ink down his spine. His skin was clear as morning dew and eyes the same color as the violets that grew in her garden. She knew she hated them for a reason.

"Is that any way to speak to a Lord?" He grinned, making good effort to show off his teeth. Pointed, long. Perfect for a demon like himself. Predator to any creature, mortal or otherwise.

"Apologies, Lord Nav." She tucked a leg behind her, a mockery of a bow. She didn't lower her head, unwilling to expose herself in such a way.

"Much better. And yes, the crpy was my doing." He sat in the front row pew as if he belonged there. Truth be told he looked regal sitting there. Perhaps the beauty of the temple would make him repent of his sins?

She was one to talk.

If she was quick enough the pike in her bag could be through his chest in a matter of moments. But he would be upon her before she could even open the flap. She had tried it once before—except the bag had been closer that time and she

45

wound up with a nasty bruise upon her spine and neck.

That wouldn't do.

Lysa looked about, taking in her position. She wasn't too far from the altar, maybe there would be something of use left there.

The candles started burning at the carpet, small flames grew about it, almost catching the golden tassels that hung from the table. *That* could become a problem.

"What purpose did he serve? You banished him rather quickly. I almost had it." She smirked. If only she had been quicker, this entire conversation wouldn't be happening.

"You stopped appearing at all your old haunts."

"*Don't* call them that." Lysa took a breath. She couldn't afford to let him under her skin.

He leaned forward, pressing elbows to knees and laced fingers to chin. "So terrible that the priest came when he did. You almost had the crpy, nice strategy."

"You heard the priest, the object is holy, no mortal should touch it. Shame my pearl flask is missing." She eyed Nav's belt, hidden under a maroon cloak. The gleam would be hard to miss if he had picked it off her person sometime between her leaving her home—which was covered in talismans—and arriving at the temple.

"Indeed, that. It is a good thing then that you are *not* mortal."

His gaze bore into hers, she hoped she burned him with hers.

Her jaw refused to let, her words struggled to bite free. "I wonder whose fault that is?"

"It is not a *fault*, darling. Nothing is wrong. You just cannot accept fate." Nav stood, brushing out the wrinkles of his buttoned shirt.

"My fate is to send you back into the *ground*." She gripped the Saints staff—it screamed in her hand. With a cry, she swept it at where his head had been a moment ago.

"Too slow my dear." His hands ghosted over her waist. She spun and struck again, dropping her hand to the bottom orb on the staff for the longest reach possible. The tip of the cross brushed a strand of hair out of Nav's face.

His eyes widened, pupils growing for a moment she would freeze into her memory. *So close.*

"Your fate, dear Lysa, is to sit by my side. Why not try and bring light to the darkness?" He ducked under her next swipe and grabbed hold of the staff, wrenching her close.

"You can't forget, a pack of crows is called a murder. And I intend to live up to my blood's calling." She landed a kick to his torso, sending him back half a step.

"I see you still are not willing to see reason yet. Very well. I shall have to try again. Goodbye, my love. Until we meet again." He crossed an arm over his chest and before she could land the cross upon his head, he was gone.

She swore as a black feather drifted down to her feet. Stuck around the middle was a golden ring, a marquise onyx set in the middle of it. A beautiful piece that cradled her ring finger perfectly.

She plucked the ring up and buried it in her pocket. The

feather she twirled about in her fingers a moment before stuffing it beside the ring. It was a shame her own never looked that nice.

Caw, caw.

You're not looking. You aren't giving him that satisfaction. Lysa wet her lips, picked up her bag, and set about righting the altar she had destroyed.

Caw, caw.

Her hands pressed against the burning fibers, righting and restoring them to their prior state.

Caw, caw.

The candles were positioned upright and the leather-bound books were stacked in an order she hoped was proper. Setting the text of Saint Mooun atop the teachings of Saint Collins was an insult she was sure, but she wasn't a fan of Collins.

A smile grew on her face, painfully pulling at her muscles. Looking up at the windows she muttered a small prayer. The small smoke window on the left was opened.

Soon, the tension in her jaw melted away to let the words floating about in her mind breathe the same air as he. "Same as you, I'm not giving up. . . my dear."

Alone Together

I stare out at the light and wonder 'are you alone as I?'

For in this night where I'm lost in sight I can't help but wonder more.

Has another soul found peace as I, amid the moonlit glow? Or in the stillness of the snow, or on the subtle breeze? Is this moment just for me or do I share it with thee?

Hello far light between the trees, I wish you a goodnight.

Thoughts in
the Heavens

The stars were trying to tell her something.

Their twinkling position had to hold reason—she was sure of it. Just as she saw meaning in the petals of a daisy and the spots on a ladybug. Her thoughts had to be reflected in the sky.

And she would do well to listen.

Something She Couldn't

The leaves that once crunched underfoot were gone. Replaced by a soft airy feeling that tickled the soles of her feet.

She trailed a finger against a birch tree, wondering when green would sprout from its limbs, wondering if she would still be about to see the way the branches swayed in the golden light of morning.

The girl wandered and wandered through the woods—skipping when her heart felt the need to be as a child. All other times she walked with purpose, shoulders square, eyes searching for something to focus on.

Every detail cried out for attention, the way the leaves fell about her greying hair, or how the light refracted on a tear caught on her lashes. Or the squirrels that flew from tree to tree in a never-ending game of tag.

Everything seemed important to the girl, and all together nothing at all was.

The leaves that fell were soon to be dirt, no different than the dirt that already was. And squirrels were nothing but mindless beasts that looked to fill their gut past their limits.

Something that had not always been so in her mind. It was confusing the girl, seeing both mindsets that she'd held at different times all at once.

Enjoying the beauty of life and wondering at the marvel of it all.

And recognizing that nothing was special, nothing at all.

Not a pretty flower, not the babble of her favorite creek, not even herself. Nothing held value.

But she knew that everything did.

And she knew everything didn't.

And so she walked.

She walked the woods, enjoying the everlasting peace that would only last until the next moment when grief would overtake her once more.

But she rested in knowing that peace would come after the grief, and that was all she could give herself in these moments. The scales had tipped, and she had bathed in grief, drowned in sorrow, and embraced the darkness far more than she should.

But now light broke through for the first time. A small crack of it lit up her broken figure. And cracks had a nasty habit of spreading when they came. Of taking over the spots where darkness had glossed. Though it was too late she welcomed the realizing light. Perhaps it could aid her in some way.

For now, she could see the trees in their beauty, something

52

she couldn't before.

Now she could hum with the babbling creek, something she couldn't before.

She could laugh as the squirrels flew about, something she couldn't before.

Now she felt alive.

Something she couldn't before she died.

Unexpected

eath was not at all how she expected it to feel. She slowly rode along the currents that pulled her down, into the dark abyss of the frozen lake.

The bodies standing over her bowed and slowly pulled off the black veils she had seen moments before, adorning the crowns of their heads. Her own veil had fluttered off when she was first submerged in the depths. She wondered if the flowers pinned into her hair joined the veil, or if they stayed rooted among locks of red. Each figure pushed their dressing, with a stone resting upon the middle, into the carved hole and let go.

The veils soon sank about her, like little wisps of smoke.

She had always known this day was coming, she was born for it. Born the ever rare second daughter of the high priestess, the one that should not have survived the cleansing ritual, the perfect blessing to the god of the after. He had fought for her soul to be born, and to him, it should go.

The water grew colder, something she had not expected as

her red hair grew black around her eyes. White gown shimmering against the dark water.

The chains that wrapped about her ankles and legs melded into her skin. Her arms did not have the strength to lower from their position above her head. They had risen up so quickly after she had been dropped in.

She tried closing her eyes, not able to bear the look of the surface above her where shadowed bodies began to dissipate. Two lone figures stood atop the ice when all else vanished. She took comfort in the fact that she would not be leaving this world alone. Holding each other as lovers often did. Her sister Aspen, and her lover, Strag.

She cried when she realized she would not live to see them joined—but her sacrifice would bring the peace needed for their lives to continue as calm as silk.

Green plants wrapped about her pale form, pulling her down further, past the blocks which had stuck themselves into the mud, past the roots that entangled themselves for food, and then she twisted into open air.

Death was not at all how she expected it to feel.

 Salvation for One

The still-burning shards of tree bark scraped the bottoms of Naomi's feet. Any trace wounds they left behind would be healed in a matter of moments; along with the charred and flaking skin along her forearms and legs. This was a pathetic attempt at bringing her own death. Her spirit was woven into the nature of the world and it refused to let go.

She thought through her actions, wondering why the desire rooted in the first place.

Morbid curiosity at knowing death could be achieved, perhaps?

The feeling crept in slowly, she recognized it like one would realize an unwarranted guest was at their front door, left with no other option but to let them in for a cup of tea that never drained. So she entertained it more—poured more tea until its porcelain cup was cracking with use. After that came fine wine in a tulip glass. When that had run dry she turned to anything else to obtain some peace. She had poured herself out to the feelings of her own mortality, or lack thereof, willing it to let her alone.

It wouldn't.

The flames faded and so did her thoughts. Slowly she turned and looked back at the scorched patch of woods, still feeling stiff from being bound so tightly to a tree whose only remnants were the splinters in her spine. The thinner saplings from the small grove lay scorched and weeping on the charred ground. The stronger, elder trees at the edge of the clearing had blackened bark but overall stood proud against the rage.

A scoff broke free of her throat.

She had gone to great lengths to be discovered washing in a lake by a few villagers, a wisp of fire dancing between her fingers—a simple trick being tied into nature allowed her—she'd pretended to be startled by their discovering her. Naomi's heart almost took flight as they dragged her back to their village with cries of witch on their tongues. No sooner was she tied to a tree and left to burn was she still breathing and stepping away from the trees remains.

A set of footsteps grew close. Right on time.

"I still do not understand, Naomi, why you continue to try?" A tall man, thin and pale, dressed in a pressed white tunic and dark pants with inky hair dripping from his scalp, came up beside her. A long coat lay over his arm.

She rolled her eyes at him, withholding the urge to utter some snark reply.

He, much like the feeling of her found immortality, refused to leave her be.

Naomi blew a strand of burnt hair out of her face. "Come

now, Riven, you cannot expect me to give up on my—seven hundreth attempt?" Her voice cracked, a cough quickly escaping her lungs with a drag of smoke following it. It coated her tongue in a bitter taste. She would find a stream quick as she could to wash. Riven extended the coat towards her and she slipped into it, grateful for the coverage it gave as her charred skin grew to the peachy, raw under layers.

She hated this part.

"I believe this was your ninety-eighth hundreth. You're getting more creative." He jutted his thumb backward.

Her eyebrows shot up. "You mean the time I tied myself to a boulder the size of a demi-god and hurled myself into the sea wasn't creative? I would say that was my best work yet. Took you nearly eight hours to find me breathless amongst the bottomfeeders."

"You would have shriveled up if I'd left you any longer than that. Tell me, how much further are you willing to go in this little game you know you'll lose?"

"I'm done. I—I'm tired, Riven. I don't know why I was chosen above others, why they get to move on when they die and I'm stuck."

Naomi stomped off in the opposite direction, hopeful to find a decent place to think about what she intended to do next over a glass of whiskey or whatever strong drink this country served.

"Let's meet up again soon. Wonderful conversationalist you are!" He called after her.

She tried thrice more to perish.

Once by screeching into the tall mountains until an avalanche encapsulated her figure. Then she kicked a bear cub in the presence of its mother on her way back through the Apennine, resulting in temporary evisceration—granting her time to think as her organs patched themselves together and returned to her body. The final attempt was made by letting a blade sharper than her wit dance along the skin of her legs and arms—eventually letting it stand in her neck as she watched the wax drip off a candle until it burned dry.

Riven never showed his face. She wasn't sure if she should be concerned by his absence, whatever the reason for it. His company, she realized, was nice.

Now she sat on the edge of a fountain reflecting on the life she had before she died in some foreign village with coins that had some Caesar's face imprinted upon them. These were far different times than when she walked in Uruk. This village was filled to the brim with emerald trees and happy chattering people who didn't seem to have a care in the world.

Children danced through a market brimming with fresh fruits and goods of all kinds.

A wonderful time to be alive.

If only.

Naomi returned to her pondering, trying to picture the

happy family she knew she had or the foggy memories that took up space in her mind—but nothing she could recall gave clue as to why she was stuck here. She let a hand drift down into the shimmering water, cursing as the longing for the cool feeling it promised was denied. She cleared her mind a moment, trying to remember how water felt.

She remembered that water was always a blessing on hot summer days, but the feeling it gave as it ran over her skin was absent. Was it silky, or oddly hard for a liquid? A bout with magma proved resistance in that fluid, but water held no such properties. She could trail her hand through it effortlessly. She liked water more than magma, at least at this depth.

A cry broke through her wall of silence, followed by a trail of black smoke in the air.

Naomi half-heartedly followed the murmuring crowd that ran towards the smoke. Through a break in the trees she saw it. A beautifully ornate home lit ablaze.

Two people stood outside, slightly older looking and covered in gold jewelry. She assumed them to be the leaders of the small village.

The woman screamed and pointed to the house. "By Olympus! Abigail is still inside!" Naomi followed her finger to see a small child with bright red hair standing in the upper window, the latch of it far above her head. "Someone go get her!"

The windows of the lower floor shattered outward and the structure groaned.

"Maria, we are sorry." One of the young men clamped a

hand down on Maria's shoulders—she promptly fell weeping into his arms.

Others who stood closer to the building started to yell instructions to Abigail, but she was frozen in the blaze—wide eyes staring hopelessly down at the crowd.

"Someone, please, go get her before it's too late!" Maria cried.

It tore at Naomi's heart.

"Maria, no one could survive getting in there. Even if they could, how do you expect someone to get her out? No one can go in."

It was true. No mortal could survive that blaze, the threat of the whole structure coming down upon them.

Naomi darted towards the house, shoving off the hands that tried to stop her as she flew through the doorway. The smoke was thick and dried her eyes. The heat of the blaze warped the bit of reality she could see.

Naomi scrambled through the small area, desperately trying to find the stairs. Through a break in the black she saw the burning banister and lunged for it. She started up the steps, gripping tighter to the railings until the steps before her gave way. A burst of fire shot up as new air was introduced to it, along with being fed.

Why must life be so complicated?

She bit her lip, leaned back slightly, and threw herself forward, only just catching the base of the upper floor with her arms. She paused a moment to steady herself before pushing up into the second floor.

No flames licked the walls.

"Abigail!" She called, making her way to the room she saw the little girl's face in.

"Mama!" The girl appeared in a doorway, soot clinging to her arms and dress, a small cloth toy in her arms. "Who are you?"

"I'm here to help you, come here." She entered the room that was starting to smoke and gathered some blankets in her arms.

"The house is hot, my head hurts. I want my mama." The girl's eyes grew pink. Naomi was sure if it wasn't so dry that tears would be flowing.

"I'm going to get you back to your mother soon, okay?" She started wrapping Abigail in the blankets, "help me by pulling on as many of these as you can." Naomi peered into the hall. The fire had climbed and was approaching the room.

Yes, she very much preferred water. Fire was destructive and greedy in a way no other element could match.

She looked back and saw Abigail bundled up in at least six blankets, one looking to be filled with down. "Perfect." She moved to the window and undid the metal latch that threatened to melt her fingertips as she opened it. A surge of wind burst past her and the fire down the hall roared.

"She's made it to Abigail's room!" Someone yelled, Maria's face was flooded with relief as others seemed to whisper to themselves, huddled about.

"I'm going to throw her down!" Naomi called.

"You're going to throw—no! I don't want to!" Abigail bolted.

"You're going to be alright." Naomi easily caught her and

tightened the blankets about her. Gathering Abigail up in her arms Naomi rushed to the window. "Ready?" She called down.

A group of men had gathered as close to the house as they could in a circle ready to catch the child. "Hold tight to the blankets. Good luck, Abigail." Naomi hugged her, then threw her hard as she could. Her heart froze as she watched the child soar through the air, and it beat again as the men caught her.

She staggered a moment before she started over to the stairs. The banister was gone but the jump down to the stairs that still stood wouldn't be horrible. Righting her position she readied to jump.

The ground groaned and caved under her feet and Naomi landed hard on her front. The front wall collapsed, sealing off the windows and front door. She crawled to a clearer area inside the house and started looking for a way out. The smoke built, there was no opening. Her lungs heaved a string of curses.

Soon, her cursing gave way to laughter. It bellowed out from her belly, filled with a joy she hadn't known as a friend in a long while.

"Is this all another elaborate scheme, Naomi? Well done, if so." She turned her head to see Riven standing but a few paces away from her, a sly grin stretched across his teeth that almost gleamed in the firelight.

She laughed, collapsing onto the smoking floor, the walls of the house cracking around her. "I remember now."

"What is it exactly that you remember?" He strode over and stood above her.

She licked her drying lips. "My sister." How she couldn't before baffled her mind.

"Why is that important?" He asked as though he already knew the answer.

"She had the sweetest laugh in the world. Always wanted her hair braided like her big sisters—though it was a style reserved for married women. And I couldn't save her." She blinked, shocked at how easily the words slipped past her lips. "I couldn't save her the day my family's home burned to the ground. I got my parents out. My sister wasn't supposed to be home. We didn't know until it was too late." She sighed. The weight that crushed her shoulders started to lessen, only noticing it as it left.

Riven sat next to her. "My work is done, I think I'm going to miss you."

"Stay with me?" She blurted, jaw trembling the slightest bit.

"It won't take long, have no fear Naomi." He gripped her hand as the air around her began to warm.

A cough broke free of her lungs, a cloud of ashes and soot following it.

The air grew uncomfortable, and the tips of her fingers grew black and started wisping away.

"Thank you, Riven."

"Oh, I didn't do anything. It was all you." He cupped her cheek and started stroking it with his thumb.

She smiled as best she could back at him, looking him in the eye. "You helped."

"Rest, Naomi. You've earned it."

65

Acknowledgments

There are so many people who helped me with this project. From my family and friends who supported me and listened to me ramble, to my writing pals who dug through my pieces to help me bring up the gems within them. So, let's thank some people you don't even know by name!

Maestro, my loving cat. Thanks for all the snuggles and cheering me up when work got me down. You're the best, you're getting extra treats on launch day.

Noah, thanks for your love and support and for wondering why every piece ended sad—still don't know how that happened my love, but I'll work on that. The happy pieces are just for you.

Karthrax, thanks for all of your work on this collection, and talking with me about it way past my bedtime.

To my Fox and Harp Writers Group: thanks for listening to my stories and ideas. Thanks for all the snacks and fun conversations over walks.

Naomi and Abigail, my lovely sisters, thanks for listening to me talk about my stories when I held the remote hostage when all you wanted to do was watch Criminal Minds with me. Still, you listened and helped me with my pieces with excitement (and then we finished the episodes).

My parents, thanks for supporting me in all that I do. And yes, they wondered why everything ended sad too. It's a bad habit, again, working on that.

To my editor Chi, you did a wonderful job fine tuning my book. Thanks for catching my silly mistakes and for making this book the best it could be.

To all my beta readers, thank you for your feedback and for helping me tighten the collection to make it the best it could be.

Lucas King and Jonathan Young, your music fueled me as I wrote, inspiring several stories within this collection. Though I know it's unlikely, if you ever read this, "sup? I like your music a bunch."

About the Author

Xanna Renae says she doesn't like going outside, which is rich coming from someone who likes being outside. (There's a difference I promise). Growing up with a big family, Xanna was always playing games with her siblings and cousins, making up worlds and kingdoms that they reigned in. As she grew older her passion for storytelling never faded. She's currently giving life to the ideas in her head while she finishes her BA in Creative Writing from Southern New Hampshire University.

Xanna hopes to inspire other creatives to do what they love, even if it isn't full-time. You can find her snuggled up with her cat, Maestro, on her couch listening to music or watching Star Trek. Or you can find her on YouTube with her channel, XannasBooks, where she talks all things bookish and writing related. Or maybe, you'll find her wasting time on TikTok as WitchDoctorXanna—because *man* it's easy to get sucked into fun videos about book tropes and Dungeons and Dragons.

Have you guessed that she's a nerd yet?

Thanks Again

Thanks again for giving my collection a shot and for making it to this point in the book! If you've reached this point I would love to remind you of the importance of leaving reviews for the books you read. Truth be told I'm only adding in this note because Ingramspark requires an even number of pages and I didn't want some random blank page at the end.

So, here I am, awkwardly asking you to review my collection! Thanks for reading, go drink a glass of water.

#hydrateordiedrate